To Anna and to Carol for all their help and cheer—JH
To Mum and Dad—DT

Orchard Books, A division of Franklin Watts, Inc., 387 Park Avenue South, New York, NY 10016

Manufactured in the United States of America. Printed by General Offset Co., Inc. Bound by Horowitz/Rae. The text of this book is set in 16 pt. Galliard. The illustrations are pen and ink and watercolors, reproduced in four colors.
Book design by Mina Greenstein   10 9 8 7 6 5 4 3 2 1

Library of Congress Cataloging-in-Publication Data
Hindley, Judy. Mrs. Mary Malarky's seven cats / Judy Hindley ; illustrated by Denise Teasdale.—1st American ed.   p.   cm.
Summary: Mrs. Malarky, the babysitter, describes her seven cats, how she acquired them, and how they all left her for their own reasons. ISBN 0-531-05822-0.   ISBN 0-531-08422-1 (lib. bdg.)   [1. Cats—Fiction.   2. Baby sitters—Fiction.]   I. Teasdale, Denise, ill.   II. Title.   PZ7.H5696Mr   1989   [E]—dc19   88-25873   CIP   AC

Mrs. Mary Malarky's Seven Cats

by Judy Hindley • illustrated by Denise Teasdale

Orchard Books · New York

Mrs. Mary Malarky has seven cats. Would you believe a house with seven cats? She told me about them, when she came to baby-sit.

We were talking and drinking cocoa, when somebody with five dogs came on the television.

"Wow!" I said. "That's a lot of dogs!"

"Pooh!" said Mrs. Malarky. "Five? That's nothing. Look, how many fingers do you have? Go ahead and count them. One, two, three, four, five."

"That's just fingers," I said. "It isn't dogs."

"What about cats?" said Mrs.
Mary Malarky. "Would you believe
I've got seven cats?"

She drew some pictures of her cats, to show me.

"Now count these. One, two, three, four, five—just like your fingers—then six, then seven. See? It's not so many."

I tried to imagine it, but it was hard.

"Do all of them eat together in your kitchen?" I asked.

"Sure!" she said. "Why not? We have seven little saucers for their milk, and seven little dishes for their fish. All my cats love fish."

"That's a lot of dishes to wash," I said.

"Yes," she said. "But Mr. Malarky helps."

"Where do they sleep?" I asked. "In seven baskets?"

"Good heavens, no!" she cried. "They're individuals! Not every cat curls up beside the fire!" Then Mrs. Malarky told me the story of each one.

"Well, it's true that Moses loves his basket. That was where we found him, out in back, nestled up to Mr. M's old garden glove. We just couldn't take that glove away from him!

"Then Louise and Blanche, they came together. Each of them has a chair. That's what they're like. You'd think they were a couple of movie stars! They were Mrs. Martie's, till she left. You remember old Mrs. Martie? She went to live with that young niece of hers.

"Then Tom—well, he adopted us. That's right! We stopped for a minute by that pet shop. . . . Tom was just a kitten, but he saw us. It was clear he had his eye on us! The minute Tom got home, he found a box. You know about cats and boxes? Well, they love them. So that's Tom's favorite sleeping place, so far.

"Petal used to be the neighbors' cat. But when they moved, the truck went off without her. She was sleeping under this old blanket. I guess it still reminds her of home.

"As for Albert—he followed Petal! Albert was always hanging around by our back door. Then one day, in he came. And in he stayed.

"Sheba, our beautiful jungle cat, was the first. You never know where you'll find her— in the laundry,

on my pillow,

on any book left open.

She'll climb into an open drawer sometimes and never even notice when you shut it!

"And speaking of beds, isn't it time for yours?" So Mrs. Malarky made me go to sleep. I couldn't wait until she came again.

Meanwhile, I drew pictures, like she showed me. I drew those cats, all by myself. Moses and Petal and Tom and Louise and Blanche and Albert and Sheba.

Finally, one night she came again.

"Let's talk some more!" I said. "How are your cats? Moses and Petal and Tom and Louise and Blanche and Albert—"

"My, oh my!" said Mrs. Mary Malarky. "Albert! Petal! Tom! You won't believe it!"

"Tell me! Please!" I said.

"Let's get our cocoa, first," she said. Then she told me.

"Gone," she said. "Gone, gone. And what a story!"

"All of them?" I asked.

"No," she said. "But listen to this!

"You remember Tom. That little rascal! Well, one day my nephew, Robert, came for dinner. He brought a rubber ball—a really bouncy one— and a piece of string for Tom to chase. Tom, of course, went wild. What could we do? You just couldn't keep the two of them apart. So Tom went home with Robert.

"Then our movie stars, Louise and Blanche. Poor old dears. They were very old—great-great-grandmothers, like Mrs. Martie. But all the same, you know, I think they missed her—though they were too proud to show it, of course. One morning they were gone. Catnapped, we thought. But three days later Mrs. Martie's niece called. They'd just shown up —hungry and dirty, but purring. They weren't too old to look out for themselves.

"As for Petal, what a happy ending! Her
family came back to look for her. You should
have seen them when they found each other.
So, of course, Albert followed Petal. Well, they
had to take him, didn't they? He'd been such a
friend, through all her troubles.

"And then there was only Moses. What a mystery."

"And Sheba," I said.

"Ah, well, there's always Sheba," said Mrs. Malarky.

"What about Moses?" I asked. "What mystery?"

"Always was a mystery," she said. "Remember how he came? Just out of nowhere. He was such a wise old, tough old cat. Never really belonged to us—just stayed. Then one day, when the spring air tempted him—just went. He's probably out there now, on his own again. Hunting. Oh, but he'll be back some day.

"So Mr. Malarky got his garden glove back. And both of us got our comfy chairs back."

"Now there's only one," I said. "Just Sheba."

It seemed to me it must be sad and quiet—Mr. and Mrs. Malarky with only one cat.

"Well," said Mrs. Malarky, "not exactly. I've got a surprise for you."

Here's what it was. Count them yourself!
Yes, Mrs. Mary Malarky has seven cats. Again!

(But what if each of
those cats had kittens. . . ?)